THE SCRIPT OF
THE FINAL ESCAPE
IN THREE ACTS

Other Novels and Plays

Life is Good

A Tale of Discovery

Shelter in Place

A Case of Espionage

The Terrorist Plot

The Play of the Money Affair

THE SCRIPT OF
THE FINAL ESCAPE
IN THREE ACTS

Harry Katzan Jr.

THE SCRIPT OF THE FINAL ESCAPE IN THREE ACTS

iUniverse books may be ordered through booksellers or by contacting:

iUniverse
1663 Liberty Drive
Bloomington, IN 47403
www.iuniverse.com
844-349-9409

ISBN: 978-1-6632-7096-2 (sc)
ISBN: 978-1-6632-7098-6 (hc)
ISBN: 978-1-6632-7097-9 (e)

Library of Congress Control Number: 2025902659

Print information available on the last page.

iUniverse rev. date: 02/20/2025

For Margaret Now and Forever

With Love and Affection

CONTENTS

INTRODUCTION

This is a reprint in readable form of the script of the Play of Two Necessary Escapes. It is a three act play that combines a set of intelligent and dependable people engaged in a set of clandestine operations, that take place, figuratively speaking of course, in the United States, Europe, and the Middle East. Actually, the scenes are actually on the stage and the remainder of locations is inherent in the imagination of the viewer. The contents of the play are not make believe; they could actually happen and probably have. The play is derived from an easy to read novel entitled The Case of the Two Escapes. The characters are introduced forthwith and then again as the script progresses. There are three acts that can be adjusted by the director. Moreover, the dialog can additionally be adjusted during the familiarization process and can even be adjusted to some extent by the participants. In other words, the play is fungible. The play is suitable for a high school, college, and an appropriate community project. It also would be a good professional play or movie. This subject will not be mentioned again. That is up to the producer, the director, and the characters.

The actor scene selection in the play will be one of the best parts of the adoption. There is one additional fact. It is necessary that the proper actor is assigned to the various parts. Proper part selection is essential. Lastly for this introductory script, there is no sex, no bad language, and no violence in the play. The play is suitable for all readers. In the modern world, practically anything can be imagined. The play has some loose ends, and they are precisely to give the audience something to wonder and talk about afterwords. "Could this be really happening here or maybe somewhere else?"

Act I introduces the characters and the environment. From a design point of view, the character is who and what they are. There is no mention of their function in the play; it is developed as the drama progresses.

Act II describes the environment and the events that represent a real life situation. This act has both descriptive and real life and overtones and circumstances. There is no violence, no sex, and no bad language. You have seen this before because it sounds good and is good. However, real life characterizations and interactive behavior lend themselves to the world of the year 2025 and its everyday events. It represents what people do.

Act III enlarges on an interactive presentation with which the problem can be addressed. Thus events take place in the United States and worldwide, although the implication of other areas is relatively mild.

This play has educational benefits in the sense there are changes between the book and the play. Students of the discipline can evaluate how things evolve and provide needed insight into the manner in which society evolves. It is a good teaching tool. Happy learning. There is a good term paper residing in the subject matter. In the script, the italics items are the speaking roles of the various characters.

CHARACTERS

The characters are more important in this play than in other works in this domain. In short, what the characters do in the play is inherent in then manner they are introduced as the play progresses.

The performance centers around three people: Dr. Matt Miller, the intelligent leading character, Prof. Ashley Miller, Matt's wife, who keeps the action rolling with her wit and charm, and Dr. General Les Miller, a former outstanding military person and Matt's grandfather. All are related in one way or another.

Matt Miller, who has his PhD from a prestigious university carries the intelligence of their action. He is relatively tall, slender, and well former both physically and mentally. He is well tanned from hours on the golf course, and normally dresses like a math professor that he is.

Ashley Miller, Matt's wife, is an actress, and also professor of drama and the media. She has medium height, is beautiful looking, and wears garments and makeup like a movie actor. She wears dresses and high heeled shoes, unusual in the modern world.

Les Miller is Matt's grandfather, called the General, is a retired general officer in the military, and is slightly shorter than Matt

Miller and plays a lot of golf with him. These three characters carry the majority of the action scenes.

Margarite Pourgoine, the General's wife and called Anna for some unknown reason, is the General's wife and a professor of creative writing at the university. When she has something to say, which is not often, it is important.

Other characters are: **Harry Steevens**, a math friend of Matt's and a local policemen, **Kimberly Scott**, a government employee who handles data and is never seen but carries a serious voice, and lastly, **General Mark Carter**, who is a typical military general, perhaps a little overweight, and serves the nation as Director of Intelligence. Other characters are not specifically determined and should be selected by the producer and director based on the role they play. As an example, a college student looks like a college student.

This is a modern play. There should be no overweight actors, but people with good articulation that are pleasant to look at. The clothing, in all cases, match the role they are portraying at any point in time. For example, a man should not be wearing a tux to get a haircut and a woman should not be wearing a dress and high heels to keep house.

The subject of the play is important and the choice of an actor should not distract from his role in the play.

ACT
I

THE ENVIRONMENT OF PEOPLE AND PLACES

Scene One.

The characters are Lieutenant Buzz Bunday, The Commander, and Lieutenant Les Miller

The location is an airfield in an American war zone where combat airplanes land after a mission in the conflict. There should be a small building with a barrier for injured planes to run into for safety. Buzz should be wearing a pilot's uniform and the air force commander is wearing the uniform and insignia of a leader. Buzz is agitated because his buddy Lieutenant Miller has not returned. There is sound of flight action in the background. This is the typical method for introducing military characters.

Lieutenant Bunday: *He should be back here by now. He chased an enemy fighter plane that shot down a U.S. B-17 bomber. I told him to forget the enemy because of the amount of fuel remaining in his P-51. I got tired of waiting for him and returned here to the base to wait for him.*

Commander: *Either he has been shot down or run out of fuel. You have got 10 minutes Lieutenant. I have work to do.*

Lieutenant Bunday: *I think I hear a P- 51. His engine doesn't sound so good.*

Commander: *His engine has just cut out and he will have to make a dead stick landing.*

The sound of a P-51 running into the barrier is heard. Lieutenant Miller jumps out of his cockpit.

Lieutenant Miller: *I got him. That's 35 kills for me.*

Commander: You *both have completed your requirement of 25 missions. Report to my office at 0800 hours tomorrow.*

The Commander leaves.

Lieutenant Bunday: *That 35 gets you an air combat medal. Congratulations buddy.*

Lieutenant Miller: *Congratulations to you also. I couldn't have gotten 35 kills without you as my wing man. Maybe, you will get a medal too. I think we are the best team in the U.S. Air Force.*

Scene Two.

The characters are Lieutenant Buzz Bunday, The Commander, and Lieutenant Les Miller.

The location is the sparsely decorated Commander's military office with a door, a desk, and a file cabinet The Commander is sitting with a cup of joe and the two Lieutenants enter by the door and salute. The Commander stands up.

Commander: *At ease Lieutenants. You have completed your flight requirement and are hereby promoted to Captain, with all of the rights and privileges pertaining thereto. The Sargent will pin your Captain's bars before you leave. You will also receive Air Combat medals and Activity Bars for your dress uniform. You have two weeks leave and then report to the Pentagon for your next assignment. You will get the medals and bars in the Pentagon. Your expenses are covered by the Government. Congratulations. Captain Bunday, your English promotion is the same. Dismissed, and lots of luck. It was a pleasure working with you. One more thing. We have a transport leaving at 1300 hours that will get you directly to the states. What you do when you get there is your business, but enjoy yourself. You are the best team I have commanded in my 10 years in the military.*

There is a brief moment of eerie silence.

Captain Miller: *You are our best Commander, as well. We couldn't done it with your knowledge and guidance. Thank you.*

This is the end of combat for the two pilots. They both shake the hand of the Commander, and hesitantly leave the office.

_____

_____

_____

_____

_____

Scene Three.

The characters are Captain Les Miller and Captain Buzz Bunday on leave in New York City.

They are walking down 1st Avenue with the Statue of Liberty on one side and the Empire State Building kind of on the other side. They are looking at the girls and talking about how nice the United States is. The men stop and are discussing New York and the Statue of Liberty. Two very pretty girls pass. The men turn around to look at them, as men sometimes do. The girls know they are being looked at by military officers and are more than proud. They don't say a word, but stop for a few seconds.

Captain Buzz Bunday: *I am amazed by the quality of life in America. The food is so good and girls are beyond belief. Is the whole country like this? I should move here.*

Captain Les Miller: *It's even better Buzz. It gets better as we walk around in upper Manhattan. That's where the real slick girls are. There are even dance halls. It's too bad about our destination of Washington DC and the Pentagon. I wonder what is going on. I think we are more important than we think. I guess the big shots finally realized that they don't know everything. I have to say that flying in combat is quite an experience. I glad we are finished with it. Twenty five missions is quite a load; I'm really tired - down deep in my soul.*

Captain Buzz Bunday: *I feel unusually tired too. I'm really glad we are finished with aircraft combat and hope they don't change their mind. Do you have any idea of what we will be doing?*

Captain Les Miller: *By the way they are handling us, I think it is top secret. But who knows; everything is top secret these days.*

Captain Buzz Bunday: *Like when you ask where the bathroom is. You might get the answer, "Why do you want to know?" That would be a good place to hide something.*

Captain Les Miller: *I wish this war were over. Everything is rationed: gas, food, sugar, butter – oh that's food. They collect tin foil from candy bars, if you can find one. Also, nylon stockings to give to women in the war zone. They didn't even wear them before the war. You can't buy a car. You can't find cigarettes and have to resort to that roll-your-own brand. People all over are buying $25 war bonds to help with the cost of the war. You pay $18.75 for them and they are worth $25 when they mature. Even the automobile workers are being used in the factories to make bomber planes and fighter planes. There is one place, I think in Cleveland, where they can turn out 16 bombers in one day. They even have women working. I've heard they are good. They have a name but I can't remember it.*

Captain Buzz Bunday: *Where do you hear about all this stuff?*

Captain Les Miller: *Letters from home, and they even sensor them. If your script is bad enough, the sensors can't read them, and they pass them through. They think that if they can't read them, the enemy can't either.*

Captain Buzz Bunday: *Wow. Holy smoke. Look at those two nice looking chicks. They are heading right to us. They look interested.*

Captain Les Miller: *They are looking at us. It's too bad we have to go the Washington tomorrow. I think the train leaves at 6:30 AM. We had better hit the hay. No girls for us.*

This is the end of New York and the girls for the two P-51 pilots, who are now Captains.

_____

_____

_____

_____

_____

Scene Four.

The characters are military officers in dress uniforms, scientists, Professors, the Commander and newly promoted Captains Miller and Bunday.

The scene is a conference room in the Pentagon. There are slogans all over the walls. The chairs are arranged in a in complicated form of disarray. There are officers, scientists, professors, and math people sitting around in some random form and there is a table at which the Commander will be sitting. The military men are dressed smartly in their dress uniforms and the remainder aren't in any particular form of dress. It would appear that the men who have the most to say are dressed the worst. They all act like they are the world's smartest people. Yet they have not been able to solve the problem of the high number of P-51s that have been shot down. They have tried amour plating and it hasn't worked. This problem has been going on for some time and the men are frustrated. The wall has a substantial door. Then the Commander comes in with Captain Les Miller and Captain Buzz Bunday. The men in the room are talking like they own the world but quiet down when the Commander comes in. The non-military characters are any old form of man. The precise number of men is not established.

Commander: *Attention gentlemen. I would like to introduce Captain Miller and Captain Bunday. They are back from the war zone. They are to be congratulated. They will receive Air Combat medals and Activity Bars.*

A military aid pins the Air Combat medals and Activity bars onto the uniforms of Captain Miller and Captain Bunday. The audience claps, but rather weakly. Captain Miller and Captain Bunday have big smiles on their faces. They are proud.

Commander: *They are here to assist us with the problem that too many P-51s are being shot down in ordinary bombing missions. We, as a strategic force in the war, cannot sustain the fact that a high failure rate of 90% of the P-51 aircraft cannot be sustained in terms of personnel and aircraft.*

The Commander displays P-51 photographs showing various angles of the aircraft that have returned.

Commander: *We have tried to armor plate the planes with titanium and it didn't seem to make a difference. We have selected all clean areas on the aircraft for armor plating.*

Captain Miller: *I can solve your problem gentlemen, and reduce the failure rate to roughly 10% which I can imagine would be satisfactory.*

A scientist stands up.

Scientist: *The Captain is off his rocker. There are professors, scientists, and Generals here that can't solve the problem and a recently promoted Captain says he can solve the problem. He is totally crazy.*

All of the men in the room just laugh.

Commander: *Let's take a coffee break gentlemen and take up the problem again in 10 minutes.*

Captain Les Bunday: *Are you out of your mind? You are going to get us demoted on our first day as Captains.*

Captain Miller: *Don't worry Buzz. I'll take care of it.*

Captain Bunday: *What did you major in at college?*

Captain Miller: *Math. Don't worry about it.*

_____

_____

_____

_____

_____

Scene Five.

The characters are The same as scene four.

The other men come back into the room and take their seats. Most of them are laughing. Some just look dejected.

Captain Bunday. *I hope you are right buddy.*

Commander: *Did you want to continue Captain Miller?*

Captain Miller stands up.

Captain Miller: *Thank you. The objective of this meeting is to determine where titanium plates should be placed for protection of the P-51s with bullet hole damage. Here some photos.*

Captain Miller holds up some photos.

Captain Miler: *The photos show P-51s with bullet holes. The planes have been plated where the holes are with no improvement. That's the reason we are here. It's an easy problem.*

The rest of the audience just laughs. Another officer speaks:

An Officer: *The guy is an idiot. I thought the reason they are here is to help us. The new Captain is totally off his rocker. This is a tough and important problem, and we need to solve it as quickly as possible.*

Captain Miller calmly continues.

Captain Miller: *It's easy gentlemen. The important holes went down with the plane – in fact – probably caused it. Look at the photos, do* *you see any planes with holes in their bellies. We should be plating areas where there are no holes.* I repeat, places with no holes. They bring down the aircraft.

The audience in the room just looked at each other. That was the solution to their problem.

Captain Miller continues. No one says a word.

Captain Miller: *If the Army Air Force would armor plate the untouched areas, evident in the photos that we have, then the problem will be solved. For identification, we can call the operation 'Reverse Mathematics.'*

_____

_____

_____

_____

_____

Scene Six.

The characters are The same as scene four.

This scene is subsequent to scene five. Some time has passed. The members of the group file back into the military room. The same room as scene five, but the organization is different reflecting a later time period. The commander takes the stage, so to speak.

The Commander: *This will be a short meeting, gentlemen. We all have work to do, and I know your time is limited. I am pleased to announce that Captain Miller's solution named reverse mathematics has reduced the problem. The amour placed in clean aircraft bellies and the percentage of shot down P-51s was reduced to 10%.*

The audience just looked at the two Captains with pleasure, and some of them offered a handshake.

The Commander: *Captions Miller and Bunday. Attention! You are now promoted to the rank of Major in the Army Air Force with all the privileges pertaining thereto. This is a bit unusual, but we are all operating in unusual times. The number of saved men and aircraft was quite large, and it noticeably changed the nature of the combat operation. Congratulations.*

Insert for the reader:

This is a true story. The author has researched the subject and read the descriptive math paper that describes it. It was termed reverse mathematics here for lack of a better name. A distinguished professor eventually worked on it for some time and named it survivorship bias.

Reference:

Ellenberg, J., How not to be Wrong. New York: Penguin Press, 2014, p. 3-9.

———————————————————————

———————————————————————

———————————————————————

———————————————————————

———————————————————————

Scene Seven.

The characters in this scene are Les Miller, now a Colonel in the Army Air Force, a driver that is a Sargent called Bud in the Army Air Force, and a beautiful young woman whose light military vehicle has run off the road in rural England. The U.S. jeep is on the audience left and pointing in that direction. The truck is at an angle off the road and the woman is standing at the edge of the muddy road. She is located at the audience right, about 20 feet from the men. She is wearing a British female military uniform.

Miller's job is to check returning P-51 flights and perform an assessment of damage imposed by the enemy. Then based on necessary analytics, initiate protective measures available from aircraft vendors. Then, go to their next air base and do the same thing. The travel between bases is treacherous, and it is often necessary to eat K rations and sleep in a pup tent. The K rations are good and include a chocolate bar and a pack of Lucky Strike cigarettes. The officers also have nylon stockings to give to the local residents, even though they probably did not have them beforehand. The relationship between U.S. military men and English folk is quite good.

Miller driven by Bud pass the women for security reasons and then back up to offer assistance. She is a Second Subattern, I.e. a second lieutenant, in the women's auxiliary corps.

Colonel Miller: *Are you okay?*

The Woman: *I'm just a bit frightened. I've been off the road for a long while, and thought that no one would show up to assist me. You are Americans?*

Colonel Miller: *We are both Americans. Let us help you.*

The jeep, a remarkable little vehicle, pulls her out of the mud and the conversation continues.

Colonel Miller: *We are traveling between cases; we work on airplanes.*

The Woman: *You are a Colonel. Do you fly airplanes? My name is Mary Wales, by then way.*

Colonel Miller: *I am a pilot. My name is Les Miller and my driver is Sergeant Bud Small. By the way, would you like some chocolate, or cigarettes, or nylons. We have chocolate and cigarettes from our K rations, and they give us nylons to give to women we encounter. We know that some times are not available in England.*

Mary Wales: *I would appreciate some chocolate and nylons. I am very hungry and have been waiting here, off the read, for a long time.*

Bud Small: *Are you sure you don't want cigarettes?*

Mary Wales: *No thank you. I don't smoke. Smoking is bad for you.*

Bud Small: *That's probably true. Some people don't care. We don't smoke either. That's why we have them to give away.*

Colonel Miller: *You are very brave. Most women don't want to help out with the war effort. You look like my sister. She is very beautiful.*

Mary Wales: *Thanks for the complement. Can I give you a good old British hug?*

Colonel Miller: *Sure, and I'll give you an American hug in return.*

Mary Wales and Colonel Miller give each other a hug.

Mary Wales hesitates. *Miller wonders why. He looks up.*

Mary Wales: *This is the first hug I have ever been given. People don't touch me.*

The remark is left unanswered and the two vehicles proceed in opposite directions.

Colonel Miller: *Nice looking girl. I hope she makes it wherever she is going.*

Bud Small: *You bet.*

_____

_____

_____

_____

_____

Scene Eight.

The characters are Matthew Miller, usually referred to as Matt and Ashley Wilson are both students. A Professor named Marguerite Purgoine, known as Anna is also in the scene. There are also students seated in a medium sized room, lined with books.

The scene is a stairway on the left, an open door, and a small classroom filled with students looking outward. Two seats are free. The two students, Matt and Ashley, are trudging up. The young man - i.e., Matt begins the conversation.

Matt: *Hi, my name is Matthew Miller, but most people call me Matt. Are you going to make it?*

Ashley: *Well, I think so. I'm not so Athletic, my Mom wanted to be a soccer mom, and now I hate running and exercise of all kinds. My name is Ashley Wilson.*

The couple plough upward until they reach the apartment. The door is open wide to a large studio with bookshelves and thousands of books scattered practically everywhere. The professor is standing just inside the door, and lets them in. Then professor is a small woman with gray hair and the softest skin on this side of the Mississippi. She is called Anna. The floor is flat the a stairway is simulated by the students actions.

Anna: *Welcome to creative writing.*

The couple grab the two remaining seats. Comment: This is a bit hard to envision, but it can be done. The audience is busy looking at the young students, anyway.

Anna continues: *You are in the most worthwhile course that you are going to take at this prestigious university. My name is Marguerite Purgoine and I will be your teacher. In the class and with email and messaging, I would prefer that you call me Anna – heaven only knows where that name came from. On the street and in the university, please call me Professor Purgoine or Dr. Purgoine. I am well aware of grade inflation throughout the country and especially this campus. So just do your job and I will take care of you.*

Matt and Ashley smile at one another. Matt and Ashley become close friends and eventually get married.

Matt and Ashley turn out to be major characters in the play. In this scene, they are dressed as students.

_____

_____

_____

_____

Scene Nine.

The characters are Les Miller, Army Air Force Three Star General Officer, obtained through outstanding military achievement, former Three Star General and Nuremberg War Trial lawyer Bill Donovan, and two Iranian graduate students. (Just mentioned.)

In spite of an enormous contribution to the U.S. Army Air Force, General Miller encountered a major problem. The number of enteral officers is governed by congress. No slots were available for General Miller to be promoted to a Four Star General until someone retired. There is a time limit. If a slot is not available in that time limit, then then he must retire. There are ways to extend the time limit. This is the Army way. Further education is one method for extending the time limit, and Miller used it wisely.

At first, Miller contacts Donovan about the problem and a possible alternative. It starts with a telephone call between the two officers.

General Miller: *That's the problem Bill. It looks like I will have to retire. I don't see a solution for me to get my fourth star. This is peace time and things are tight. I've done some really speculative things in my career, like save a plane load of general officers and work with you on the Nuremberg trials. Someone owes me something; that's what I think, anyway.*

Donovan: *I know where you are going with this Les. It happened with me also. I took the retirement as a 3-star and got a law background. Actually, I had the Army support my law training. I'm a JD. That* ended, and now I am the President of a university in Brooklyn, and we have a new Computer Science program. You can get a Master of Science degree in CS in a year. By then, something may open up while you are in school. If not, maybe you can add another school to the list. We have the best master's program in the world. One of the faculty wrote a bunch of books, and that served to kick our program off. I even got them a new computer. There is money all over the place. Especially in politics.

General Miller: *I think I will go with that Bill. Perhaps I can use that knowledge to build a new business or something when I really do retire. I also wanted to get flight certified on the B-29.*

Quick change to scene ten. Lights off and then lights on. It's a way to emulate "a few years later', actually only one.

_____

_____

_____

_____

_____

Scene Ten.

The characters are Les Miller, Army Air Force Three Star General Officer, obtained through outstanding military achievement, former Three Star General and Nuremburg War Trial lawyer Bill Donovan, and two Iranian graduate students.

This is a telephone conversation between General Miller and Bill Donovan, President of the University. Miller is about to finish his Master of Science program, and has been accepted in a PhD program, along with a slot in the B-29 training program. He is still waiting for a slot open in the Four Start General rank, and his advisor has pulled a few strings to keep Miller in the system. A few years ago, Miller had saved a plane load of General officers and apparently that meant a lot. Actually, Donovan pulled the strings and he is not letting Miller know that.

General Miller: *Hello, Bill. This is Les.*

Donovan: *Hi Les. I know it is you; it's on my phone. Modern technology is wonderful. Congratulations. I heard of your success. I have some news that you haven't heard of yet. They are holding the B-29 course during your summer vacation in that PhD program. They have divided it into two sections.*

General Miller: *It's the best we can do. If the slow doesn't open up in that time, I guess that I am going to bail out. Those Iranian students named Robert Peterson and John Evans want to get into a PhD program in math at Cal Tech. Can you help them?*

Donovan: *I have already. They do not know it yet. Just tell them who you are. They will be your friend for years. I gotta go, Les. We have a big campus meeting and I am the person running the show. Tell them they are in at Cal Tech, and you can juice it up a little by telling them you had something to do with it. Over and* out.

The Iran students are graduate assistants, and have an office of their own. Les Miller walks over to their office and tells them the result. They are overjoyed and invite Miller out to dinner. Then Miller tells them that he is an active military General and they are totally surprised.

_____

_____

_____

_____

_____

A PROBLEM IS DETERMINED

Scene One.

The characters are Matt and the General.

The characters have settled in to their respective routines. Dr. Matthew Miller is established himself as a first-rate mathematician, The General has earned his masters and doctorate degrees and has been certified as a B-29 pilot, He has been successful in business and is settled in as a person that enjoys helping people. Buzz Bunday is active in England as a member of the British Secret Service (BSS), Ashley is married to a member of British Society, but they have gone their separate ways. The General is Matt's grandfather, but are generally regarded as associates.

The general has called Matt on the telephone. The stage is dark with the two lighted telephones at either end. The scene has already been set.

The General: *Matt, something has come up. Can we meet for dinner? I know you will say yes. How about tonight at 6:00 in the Green Room? I'll get us a private booth at the rear of the dining room.*

Matt: *It must be serious. You couldn't A tell me what it is about., could you?*

The General: *Nope.*

Matt: *I'll be there.*

The lights flick off for a few seconds, and then the lights are turned on with the stage set. The General is seated at a private booth. Matt arrives and sits down at the table in the booth. The stage was set before the previous phone conversation.

The General: *What are you having?*

Matt: *That new non-alcoholic beer called Zero. What are you drinking?*

The General: *Scotch. You are a big drinker.*

The waiter is waiting.

The General: *Scotch on the rocks and a Zero. We will order in a few minutes.*

Matt: *I don't have anything against drinking alcoholic beverages. I just never got started. It was also that way in college.*

The General: *Have you heard of the new computer database methodology called Blockchain?*

Matt: *I didn't know you were up to date on that stuff. Of course, I know about it.*

The general: *I never told you about computers and me. It is one of those things I never talked about. I have a Master of Science in Computer Science from Pratt Institute in Brooklyn. The institute has since decided to concentrate on art and design.*

Matt: *How in the world did you end up there?*

The General: *One of my former associates at OSS is the President there. He said they had a new Master of Science degree there, first in the world, and I enrolled there. And got the MS. I have a sad story about Gary Powers who was a military pilot and involved with the the President. He was flying for a California TV station. The chopper had a faulty fuel gauge that contained a nominal amount of fuel when the gauge read empty... Someone fixed the fuel gauge, so Powers thought there was fuel in the tank when it really empty. He crashed and died. That was an unfortunate case. I used my knowledge of computer knowledge to start up my political polling business. This happened when I was in the military waiting for a promotion. I also got a PhD in international relations from Princeton, all when I was waiting for a promotion from Lieutenant General, that is 3-star, to a General, that is 4 star.*

Matt looked at the General straight in the eye.

Matt: *That is some story. But I know you are stalling for some reason. What is it?*

_____

_____

_____

_____

_____

Scene Two.

The characters are Matt and the General.

The previous scene is kept the same.

The General: *Well, it is important and it might involve your friend Ashley.*

Matt: *What has she done? Maybe I should ask if she is okay.*

The General: *Well, she is okay, and the situation doesn't involve her directly. I think. Have you heard from her?*

Matt: *Yes. She messaged me yesterday. She's in London and wants to re-marry that Prince Michael to whom she was previously married. She wants to come back to the states where he could be a Professor. He has since received his PhD from Oxford. It's not clear whether or not he knows about this. I replied with almost nothing, but I humored her to the best of my knowledge. And that's it.*

The General: *Here's the story. I received a satellite call from my old Army buddy Buzz Bunday. The Royal Family, as least the Queen and Prince Michael, know about someone known as the General who is good at solving problems of a complicated nature. However, the BSS, as a group, does not specifically know about the interest by the Queen in complicated problems, and also about me. The Queens needs someone to solve a major problem and probably some minor problems. This is another situation that could have been prevented. The record keeping in the Monarchy is poor and any checks and balances that would normally occur do not exist. That's it.*

Matt: *I think your want me to go there, and you want me to accompany you - perhaps to solve the record keeping problem.*

The General: *That's what I had in mind. Perhaps, I could solve the major problem, and you could take care of the other one.*

Matt didn't say a word. He didn't like minor problems and the General was no ace in solving major problems. He just sat there thinking what to say.

Matt: *How long?*

The General: Probably fourteen days; maybe fifteen, but definitely not less than ten. We could take the Gulfstream and land at London City Airport. We would have to give our real names, but there doesn't appear to be a downside to that.

Matt: *Okay, just give me time to pack.*

The General: *I'll call Buzz, but there is one more sensitive thing I have to tell you.*

Matt: *I hope I'm not too surprised.*

The General: *It's another kind of surprise. You're not the only doctor in this room.*

Matt looked around.

The General: *It's me. I received a PhD in international relations from Princeton. I got it right after I passed the B-29 pilot certification. I'm on my way to obtain a general officer upgrade.*

Matt: *Well, I'll be. You have a bachelors, masters, and doctorate. Do you have any other more surprises?*

The General: *Let's eat. We've already done a lot of work.*

Matt just looks at him.

_____

_____

_____

_____

_____

Scene Three.

Characters: The characters are Matt, the General and Buzz Bunday, the former wing man to the General. The Queen and Prince Michael are referred to.

Same setting as scene two.

The General is returning Buzz's call.

The General: *What are you doing these days, Buzz? How in the devil did you get involved with the crown, or should I say the Queen?*

Buzz: *I'm retired and enjoying life. The connection to the Queen is through my son, who is part of the BSS, and my son's connection is through Prince Michael, who is doing diplomatic service in the BSS. They only contacted me to see if I knew who the General is. I have not responded as yet, so here is my question, "Should I tell them who are and endeavor to establish a link between you and the Queen? If so, how do you want me to make the connection?"*

The General: *Just tell them who we are and tell us when to get there. My team will be Dr. Les Miller, former a General in the U.S. Army Air Force, and Dr. Matthew Miller, mathematics professor. We can give the United Kingdom 14 days of consulting time, plus or minus a day, and there will be no consulting fee or other business expenses.*

Buzz: *What is this Dr. Les Miller? I haven't heard of that.*

The General: *I earned it after I finished my B-29 pilot certification.*

Buzz: Okay buddy. I'll let you know where and when.

Matt and the General sit there looking at Matt's new satellite phone. Buzz returns the call.

Buzz: *She will expect you at the palace gate at 9:00 AM three days from now. I can arrange for transportation from London City Airport and support your needs while you are there. I have some power around the BSS.*

The General: *That was a fast response, Buzz. It must be an important problem.*

Buzz: *The Queen thinks it is. I don't have a clue as to what it is all about.*

The General: We will be arriving at the London City Airport in the Gulfstream. I'll let you know the details. Thanks, Buddy.

Buzz: *A pleasure, Buddy.*

The General tells Matt the details.

The General: We will arrive at the London City Airport on Wednesday in the afternoon, and sleep on the plane. We will need transportation to the palace at approximately 8:30 AM on Thursday. All other arrangements will be left as open items to be addressed after meeting with then Queen.

_____

_____

_____

_____

_____

Scene Four.

The characters are the General, Matt, the Queen. The Queen is dressed in a bright green dress with suitable jewelry. Then men are dressed in black suits, white shirts, and black ties.

With the curtain closed, a pair of elves is holding the following sign with a green border to the audience:

Her Royal Highness the Queen
Announces the Following Visitors
To the Royal Monarchy

General Leslie Miller, PhD
United States Army Air Force

Professor Matthew Miller, PhD
Distinguished Mathematician

The team will be assisting the Royal Family
In the operation of The Royal Kingdom

They are a distinct honor to The Royal Family

The curtain opens to a distinguished royal meeting room. The Queen is seated, and rises when the General and Matt are escorted in to the meeting room. They offer a bow and it is waved off by the Queen. The Queen is very sophisticated and comfortable with her position as leader of the Monarchy.

The General looks at the Queen, and the Queen look at the General. They say at the same exact time:

The Queen and the General: *Do I know you?*

The Queen and the General give each other a big American hug and the Queen says:

The Queen: *I can still taste that chocolate bar that you gave me on that forlorn road during the war. I was so hungry. I saved the nylons that you gave me and I still have them.*

The General: *When I saw you on that lonely road, I thought you were the prettiest girl I had ever seen. I still do.*

Matt looks at the two of them with awe.

The Queen and the General discuss their lives.

The Queen: *My father was the King and I took over when he died. I am very busy with approximately 300 appearances in a year. One of the characteristics of being Royalty is that no one is allowed to touch you. You were the first person that has done so when we met on that lonely road. No person has touched me after that meeting on the muddy road.*

The General: *I have also been busy with being a pilot and an Army officer. Being an Army officer is a bumpy road, but I will not abstain from giving you an occasional American hug — but not in public.*

The Queen and the General move on to the current problem facing the Royal Monarchy. And the reason for their meeting.

The Queen: *We have a terrible financial problem. Someone, we know not who, has been transferring funds from several royal accounts. We don't know who that is because there are ample funds for every Royal's needs and desires. We found out about the situation from the Royal Auditor who noticed that the receiver of the transferred funds was the same numbered account. We initiated a search for the person requesting the bank transfers and it turned out to be my daughter, Princess Amelia. The Royal Auditor asked her about the bank transfers, and she indicated that it must be a mistake. She said that she had ordered none of them. There is an element of trust among royalty in that one person does not question another's integrity. I do not to bring in the police or security services since they have tendency to entertain the media with just about everything, resulting in a royal scandal. We would like to We should like to avoid a major scandal for any reason.*

The General: *What are the amounts of the bank transfers and how often do they occur?*

The Queen: *I can get that information for you. I also have the numbered account number right here.*

The General: *Do you have a general record of all financial transactions that occur — something like a ledger?*

The Queen: *We don't have anything like that. We pay no taxes, have no driving licenses, and require no identification of any sort, such as a passport. We have no need to save information.*

The General: *It is remarkable that you have a closed society, as you have in the Royalty, but in this case, it is counter-productive. That is* precisely why we have Dr. Matt Miller with us. There are methods for keeping track of any such incidents, and Matt can set it up for you.

The Queen: *Well, okay then. I suppose we need something like that.*

The General: *We can and will take care of both problems. I will need access to your Royal Auditor. Matt will take care of the operational situation. I can guarantee to you that we will be practically transparent. Matt will need access to the auditor and your data processing people. I think we can wrap this up in a week or 10 days.*

The queen was pleased. Matt was impressed with the situation.

_____

_____

_____

_____

_____

Scene Five.

The characters are the Queen, the General, and Matt, plus an entourage of English royalty at the royal dinner table.

The scenes are the Royal dining room on a bright sunny Sunday; the Queen's suite on a miserable weather Monday; a pleasant day on Tuesday; and a trip home for a few round of golf on Wednesday.

The General returned from Zurich with the financial problem solved, and the Queen requested that the General and Matt accompany her to church on Sunday followed by the royal family dinner in the palace. The scene is the royal dinner table without verbal communication. It is intended to be entertaining. Displaying English customs.

The seating is carefully prepared as is the dinner. The General sits on the right of the Queen and Matt on her left. The person on the right occupies the preferred seat. The scene opens with the royal family around the table in pleasant conversation. The meal of soup, fish, roast beef, and treacle pudding is served and eaten. There is no conversation, but an unusual demonstration of the group having a pleasant meal. No work is performed on Sunday. This is not a normal scene, but establishes the power of the royalty

_____

_____

_____

_____

_____

Scene Six.

The characters are the Queen and the General.

The General enters the Queen's suite and attempts to bow. The Queen waves him off, as usual.

The General: *Your financial problem has been solved through associates in private banking in Zürich Switzerland. We have identified the royal person involved …*

The Queen interrupts the General.

The Queen: *I am pleased to announce that Princess Amelia has been assigned to the position of Royal Deputy to the British Ambassador in Australia. She left by private plane on Saturday night after the events in Switzerland. Since I run this operation out of London and have supreme power, I made a quick decision. There will be no more surprise expenditures under my watch.*

The General: *Do you mean that you knew that Princess Amelia was the source of the problem all along?*

The Queen: *No, I did not., but I had my suspicions. The death of her husband and your computer results in Zürich confirmed everything. You must remember that in the system of British Royalty, the Monarch is the supreme leader.*

The General: *I am surprised but pleased at your success.*

The Queen: *And now, one more thing. Would take me on a date tomorrow? I know this is common among Americans, but not for Royalty.*

The General: *I would enjoy doing that. Would you like me to make a plan for the day?*

The Queen: *I would be pleased if you did so.*

The General: *I do have one more item for your knowledge and approval. Matt has totally redone your accounting operation using a new method named Box Chain in which all operational details is recorded for your safety and approval. Your staff loves it and you can rest in total satisfaction.*

The Queen: *I will award him a special Royalty medal and a case to display it. He can display it in his university office of he so desires. In case you are wondering, you will receive one as well. Many thanks from the Monarchy team.*

_____

_____

_____

_____

_____

Scene Seven.

The characters are the Queen and the General.

The scenes are the royal limousine, Harrods, Ritz Hotel, Simpson's on the Strand, and the royal limousine.

Mini scenes depict the activities of the Queen and the General at the various venues. (May be comical. Director's alternative.). This scene may be optional.

Mini scene #1. The Queen and the General in the plain limousine.

Mini scene #2. The Queen and the General at Harrods, and a little gift. (Black ball pen.)

Mini Scene #3. The Queen and the General at Ritz Hotel having a drink.

Mini Scene #4. The Queen and the General at Simpson's on the Strand.

Mini Scene #5. The Queen and the General in the plain limousine.

Mini Scene #6. The Queen giving the General a sophisticated kiss.

_____

_____

_____

_____

_____

Scene Eight.

The characters are the General and Matt.

Matt and the General are on the return flight. Both are looking forward to a few pleasureful rounds of golf. Also, a special dinner at the Green Room was something they both looked forward to, along with their wives. Matt was in good spirits.

Matt: *I never asked, but how much do we get for this job. I worked the total night with that ancient accounting system. The existing system was a copy from the Stone Age. They are up to date now and should be okay for quite a long while.*

The General: It was gratis. I forgot to tell you. Sorry.

Matt: *No wonder we got medals. You just liked the Queen.*

The General: *I made that commitment to Buzz before we left for London. Are you going to display your medal and its case in your office?*

Matt: *Do you mean at home or at the university?*

The General: *I was thinking of the university.*

Matt: *I suppose it will be the university. At home it would have to compete with the golfing trophies in the closet. Just joking.*

The General: *I think we should up our golf dates from 2 per week to 3 per week. We can work it out. I don't know about you, but I feel I am getting a little rusty.*

Matt: *Your scores are good, so I don't feel you are actually rusty. Are you feeling rusty or just bored with the same old course? Maybe you should switch to bocce, croquet, or pickleball. They are popular these days. Then there is always fishing. Or swimming.*

Matt had a grin on his face.

Matt: *Then there is always girls. The Queen really liked you. There are a lot of 40+ ads these days.*

The General: *That's not funny. I was just being professional. She's a grand dame, and you know it.*

Matt: *I know that, and that you were just being accommodating. You are very nice about things like that. I need a nap.*

Both the General and Matt take a short nap. They had worked hard and deserved it.

_____

_____

_____

_____

_____

Scene Nine.

The characters are still Matt and the General.

As the scene open, they are both asleep in three seats. Nothing has changed from the previous scene. The General's satellite phone rings and he answers it. He listens for about 5 minutes and hangs up.

The General: *That was Director Clark. There is a national emergency. They have been tracking us. Since we are about 4 minutes and 30 second outside of the New Jersey Airport, they decided to send a Presidential plane to the airport. When we land, we should go directly to that aircraft. It will be running and waiting. They will take care of luggage. We will have an emergency flight to Dulles, and a Marine One chopper will have its blades moving for our trip to the White House. No information is available on this operation. We will be briefed in the President's Office. This is* TOP SECRET.

_____

_____

_____

_____

_____

Scene Ten.

The characters are the General, Matt, Director Mark Clark, the President, The President's special assistant George Benson, also with additional characters such as airline pilots (the Airplane Captain), and other White House personnel.

Back in the Washington area, Air Force One, the President's jet plane was being readied for a fast unplanned trip. The President and Vice President were being readied for a quick trip. Having both the President and Vice President on the same flight was against regulations, but the President overruled them. This was slightly before Matt and the General had finished their work in London. The Presidential staff on the flight were minimal. The purpose of the flight and ensuing events are covered later.

This scene starts here. Matt and the General hurry off of the Gulfstream and hurry to the Presidential jet. The engines are running.

The General: *What took you so long?*

The Airplane Captain: *We are just slow people General. Good morning.*

The General: *I suspect that you don't know what is going on.*

The Airplane Captain: *Not a word. Jump in; we're late.*

The flight to DC is smooth and fast. Air traffic had been averted for their flight, reflected in their flight plan, so the trip was as fast as they could possibly make it. Marine One is waiting with its rotors running. They land in the White House heliport and in 5 minutes they are in the President's private office.

Director Clark, former General and Chief of Staff, and President Kenneth Strong are there, having tracked their flight to DC.

This is a *dynamic scene* in which the stage adjusts from the Seats in the Gulfstream to the Presidential jet, to the helicopter, to the White House and the President's private office. Essentially the scene follows Matt and the General, who sit down. It appears that Matt and the General are moving, but the stage scenery is actual moving. This is original. Director Clark starts the dialogue.

Director Clark: *Mr. President, I would like to introduce Dr. Matthew Miller, known as Matt, and General Miller of whom I spoke. Gentlemen, this is President Strong.*

Matt and the General acknowledge the President without shaking his hand.

The President: *Welcome gentlemen. Thank you for coming to our assistance. You have been suggested by Director Clark, and I am sure you can solve the problem. It is actually my problem that affects the United States and possibly the whole world. Life must go on and I have to address the Security Council. He and George Benson, my lifetime assistant, will describe the situation. Thus far, we having no solution and some decisions must be made. So we wish you the best of luck. You have the assistance of the entire nation, But they don't know it yet.*

The President leaves the office rather hesitantly, looking back as he leaves.

Director Clark: *Thanks to you Matt and the General for responding to my request. This is really a big deal and even war is not this urgent. Here is the story from the beginning up until we ran out of manageable options. The description is pretty long, so hold on to your helmets.*

Matt: *I think he is serious. (To the General but load enough so that Clark can hear it.)*

Director Clark: *You're right there. Believe me. This is all true. I was there. Air Force One was readied in a hurry and the pilots were rounded up; the President and the Vice President, along with a minimal service staff, were on board and the specially designed Boeing 747 airplane was headed to California in a hurry. Having the President and the Vice President on the same flight caused some concern with the Secret Service, who were overruled by the President. The planes headed to San Jose at the maximum speed of 600 miles per hour at 40,00 feet. The President's life-long friend and former Chief of Staff was dying and the President and his friend had made a pact to be at the other's bedside if death were imminent. The friend was dying of liver disease and wasn't expected to last the day. A few hours after the President arrived, the friend passed away, and Air Force One headed back to Washington. The President always returned home to the White House every night. He never slept away from his residence. Of course, there were exceptions for international trips.*

Director Clark took a pause for a drink of water, and then continued.

Director Clark: *When the President arrived back at the White House, it was late and he retired to a separable room in the presidential suite. He didn't want to wake the First Lady, who was nursing a bad case of the flu. The next morning, the President awakened early to read the President Daily Brief (PDB) and learned the First Lady was not there. The President, used to having everything just so, went into the panic mode and called the Secret Service. The President also called his trusted advisors to an urgent secret meeting in the blue room of the White House. The instructions were: (1) Find the First Lady, and (2) Keep the search a total secret from everyone. No one is to know in the U.S. and in the outside world. The logic was that the American people would be in a panic, the stock market would take am nose dive, and the news media would turn the situation into a frenzy. Several agencies would take care of the search and not tell anyone exactly why they were doing what they were doing. The known agencies are FBI, CIA, NSA, Police Departments, Military Intelligence, and special units from the Marines and the Army. The Chairman of the Joint Chiefs of Staff, a four star general, and I were consulted in total secrecy. In less than a week of search, there was no success. That was why and when I called you while in flight. Let me take a 5 minute break and get a cup of coffee. Then I will call in George Benson, the Presidents long time assistant, and he will continue with what has been done so far.*

The Director presses a button and a team brings in coffee and some fruit breakfast snacks. The scene continues in only a few seconds.

Director's note: *This is a very long dialog. It will probably have to be dubbed in, as in movies. This may be applicable in other instances in this script.*

George Benson: *Hello, my name is George Benson. The President has asked my to solve a problem of a secret nature. I have worked for and with him for more than twenty years.*

The General, Matt, and Director Clark introduce themselves. Benson does not look impressed.

George Benson: *The problem is that the President returned from a quick trip to California and as the hour was late, decided to sleep in an extra bedroom. The President always sleeps at home when in the States. The First Lady was ill and he decided not to disturb her. After PDB, the President was told that the First Lady was nowhere to be found. Neither the First Lady nor her Secret Service Agent could be found. The President had an emergence meeting and summoned the FBI, CIA, NSA, Military Intelligence, and local Police. The White House has been thoroughly searched. The military was put on alert. Evacuation routes and traveling routes were addressed. That included every form of transportation were checked. That necessarily included airports, train stationed, automobile routes, toll stations, border control, hotels, and other establishments. Even restaurants. The President thinks she was kidnapped but the FBI said absolutely not. We are at a dead end. He said that it persisted, he would have to tell the people, and that would be an disaster.*

Matt: *We can solve your problem. It's easy. You are looking where she could or should be. You should be looking where she shouldn't be. Then we will find her, and she will probably be close by. Have you checked the wartime bunkers? The map says there is one beneath the Treasury. Let's take a look at the Treasury Building.*

_____

_____

_____

_____

Scene Eleven.

The characters are George Benson, Matt, and the General. Some Army Engineers are used as the scene progresses. The First Lady and the Secret Service are found alive and well.

On the way to the Treasury Building, the group notices there is a tunnel between the White House and the Treasury Building. Along the side of the tunnel, Matt noticed many closed and locked rooms labeled Cat Room #xx, for use by support people in the event of an attack. It was said they were stocked with water and k-rations. No keys to the rooms were known to exist.

Matt looks at Benson straight in the eye.

Matt: *You should get the Army Corps of Engineers in here and open the doors. Do it now!*

Benson surprised by such authoritative and rough talk did just that. The corp men were there is a second. (This is a play, not real life. Actually, it would probably take an hour.)

Matt: (To the engineers). *Open the first door.*

The room was empty but contained supplies and water.

Army Sargent: *Empty Sir, what should we do?*

Matt should look at the men like they are complete idiots.

Matt: *Look at the handles and see if there is a one that is a little clean.*

The Army men do that and find a clean handle.

Matt: *Open it!!*

The door is opened and there sits the First Lady and the Secret Service agent.

Matt is tall, slender, and tanned from golfing. He speaks with a calm and reassuring tone that makes a person respect him.

Matt: *We've been looking for you. A few people are getting worried. How did you get in here?*

Secret Service Agent: *I have a key from World War II in the 1940s. Several of us were stationed here. I know I don't look that old, but I am.*

Matt: *Next Ma'am, why are you here? I won't tell anyone. It's only between you and me. But don't worry, I'll fix things up for you.*

The First Lady: *I just have this awful flu and look at me. I look like a witch. I have been blubbering all over the place. I've been crying and my hair is a total mess.*

Matt says to the Secret Service agent.

Matt: *Why I the devil did you do it?*

Secret Service Agent: *Because she asked me to do it. That's my job. I am required to do whatever she requests.*

Matt goes out of the cot room and asks Benson to call the President.

Matt: *Tell him that the First Lady has been found and to come to cot room #37 with her raincoat and hat. Pronto!*

The President arrives in less than 10 minutes. Matt says to him:

Matt: *Be kind to her Mr. President. She needs you now.*

Some time later, Matt and the General meet with the President in his private office.

The President: *Thank you gentlemen. You've solved my crisis, and I will be eternally grateful. Please send me a bill for whatever amount you please.*

The General: *There is no need Mr. President. Our work is gratis.*

On the way home in the White House jet, both Matt and the General are very pleased.

Matt: *That certainly was a worthwhile trip.*

The General: *It was indeed.*

Matt: *I could use a round of golf.*

The General: *Sound good to me.*

To the Director from the Author: *Life is Good. Don't you think?*

_____

_____

_____

_____

_____

THE ESCAPE

Scene One.

The characters are Matt. The General, Ashley, and Anna. Also, a man and lady at an adjacent table.

It is morning, and Ashley is in bed and Matt is standing at the edge of the bed. He is informally dressed for the day. She is covered with bed clothes.

Matt: Would you like a cup of coffee?

Ashley rolls over and looks at him.

Ashley: *Sure, I would love a cup of coffee. I thought you were going golfing this morning with the General.*

Matt: *He cancelled out at the last minute. I have no idea of what is going on. He called this morning at six o'clock AM and said he was too busy. He asked about an afternoon time. I said okay*

Ashley: *Both he and Anna have been acting strange lately. Maybe it's old age.*

To the Audience from the Director: *Matt and Ashley are married and long time friends. The had met in Dr. Marguarite Purgoine's creative writing course when they were students. Marguarite Purgoine is referred to as Anna for some unknown reason. She is married to Les Miller, known as the General, who served in the military as a General and was a decorated officer. Matt Miller is a well known mathematician and a professor at a prestigious university. Ashley is a former actress and teaches drama at a local community college. The General is wealthy through a political polling company and likes to help people and organizations. Both Matt and Ashley are tenured full professors with a liberal amount of freedom. Matt and the General enjoy their round of golf, but the general has very little say. Finally, after the ninth hole, at the resting area and restrooms, Matt asks what is going on. The General looks and says the following:*

The General: Something has come up and they want us at the White House as soon as we are free. Let's continue discussion this evening at the Green Room. That is, the four of us.

The dinner at the Green Room was extremely pleasant, and the subject of serious problems was not discussed. A pleasant man and woman, seated at a nearby table had the following to say:

Adjacent Woman: *I wonder what those people do to pass their time. The older couple does not even have a wrinkle on their faces, and the younger couple looks like movie stars. They are all slim and tanned.*

Adjacent Man: *They must be pretty wealthy, they didn't get a check and the younger man left a tip of fifty dollars. They also have an expensive Tesla parked in front.*

_____

_____

_____

_____

Scene Two.

The characters are Matt, Ashley, Ann Clark (The Director of Intelligence's wife).

Early the next morning, Matt and the General have their usual round of golf. Matt returns home and Ashley was waiting at the door. The scene is the inside of a door in a home.

Ashley: *I received a call from Ann, and she needs to talk with me this afternoon.*

Matt: *Must be important. What's it about.*

Ashley: *Don't know. She's taking the White House jet to the Newark Airport, and I have to pick her up from there. She said she will be available at the airport at 11:30 today.*

Matt: *I'll take off and be at the driving range. It is not my business, so send me a text message when she is gone.*

Ashley: *Why are you leaving? We know each other's business.*

Matt: *No, she wants to talk to you. Otherwise, she would have mentioned me. Something has come up. I'm glad we are on sabbatical. I bet someone has something for us to do.*

The. Stage segues from home to car with a slight movement of the backdrop. (This is a unique tactic.)

Ann arrived as planned and Ashley picked her up at the Newark International Airport in Matt's Porsche Taycan electric vehicle.

Ann: *I can't hear the engine.*

Ashley: *That's because it has an electric motor.*

Ann: *Oh, I didn't know. It's hard to keep up with cars.*

Ashley: *There's a lot going on these days. With global warning and the tense international situation, there is always something new. Conflict feeds invention, just like in World War II.*

They continued to Ashley and Matt's house, and when they got there, Ann digs into the business at hand.

The scene segues into a living room. (To the director: you are making stagecraft history.)

Ann: *I'm sorry to be abrupt. I'm here on very serious business. My message to you is directly from Mark as an order from the Director of Intelligence.*

Ashley: *It must be very serious.*

Ann: *Prince Michael is gone, so is his son, The Prince of Bordeaux, named Philip George William Charles.*

Ashley: *Again?*

Ann: *Yes again. The whole British Empire is worked up like it's a major war. The U.S. Ambassador to Britain called the President at the White House, and the White House intelligence chief called Mark. They have no idea of who took them and where they are. The* *intelligence people think it is Iran, China, or Russia. It does not seem to be related to anything in particular.*

Ashley: *It is Iran. The easiest solution is usually the best one.*

Ann: *You may be right, and the intelligence people seem to agree with you. We want you to help us solve the problem.*

Ashley: *Why me? I don't know anything about international terrorism.*

Ann: *They want you to obtain knowledge of the language and the culture of Iran. Learn the Farsi language, dress like a Muslim, go to Iran to find out if the kid is there, and then bring him back. They won't know you are an American because you will have a burka over your head. The whole operation is on the QT, but I think they want Matt and the General to play foreign scientific or business people - probably middle eastern - and get Michael out. They have another plan for that.*

Ashley: *They sure are big on plans. Don't you think they should contact someone to find out if Iran did, in fact, do the dirty work first?*

Ann: *It's the government, they do what they want to do. They make the plan, choose the people, and then blame them if the plan doesn't work. They do that in business, as a matter of fact. Make up an idea. Hire a consultant and the blame her or him if it doesn't work.*

Ashley: *I'll talk to Matt and the General.*

Ann: Let me know today. Now I'm out of here. The White House jet is waiting at Newark International Airport. It's ready to go. This is our government in action. Can you drive me to Newark?

Ashley: *Sure. We can take Matt's Taycan. It's the car in which I picked you up.*

_____

_____

_____

_____

_____

Scene Three.

The characters are Ashley, Ann, and Harry Steevens.

The scene is in the driver and passenger seats of a sporty car. Ann is seated in the drivers seat and Ashley is in the passenger seat. This is a dynamic scene. The car and passenger remain still and the scenery moves. They are talking to themselves. To the audience they are just moving their lips. They pass through a small town, the entrance to the highway, and on the highway, and the highway with a policeman at the driver's window.

The dialogue to the audience starts when the car is on the highway.

Ann: *This an amazing car Ashley. Do you drive it very often. I know you have that fashionable Chevy.*

Ashley: *The Chevy is fast enough for me. Matt and the General have their boys toys and it keeps them happy. I surprised that neither of them has ever received a speeding ticket. However, I really like this Taycan and the General's Tesla. They are both a bit expensive, but if a person can afford them, they are a good buy. WATCH IT! People like to accelerate and the police are near the entrance of the highway.*

The ladies move back in their seats to simulate accelerating in the car. The siren goes off. (It's Harry, the girl chaser. Just kidding.}

Ann: *I did it. Darn. I don't think I can talk my way out of a ticket, but I do have a government driver's license. I'm looking at him from* the side mirror. He is looking at the car. He seems to really like it. I think we are okay. He is taking off his cap.

Harry: Good afternoon ladies. Nice car you have. I drove one towards the end of last year. I stopped a couple of guys, a young one and an older one, and they let me take a drive in their new car. It was amazing empty day on the turnpike, and I took it up to 120 and then backed off. That was fast enough for me. I sorry mam, I have to ask to see your driver's license.

Ann pulled out her government issued driver's license, and Harry said:

Harry: I had one of these once.

Harry looked inside the car at Ashley. Then did a double take.

Harry: Are you Matt's Ashley?

Ashley: Yes it is Harry. Do you still wear your Beretta on your right ankle?

Harry: Sure do Ashley. Never leave home without it. Have a good day ladies. And Mrs. Clark, please drive a little more slowly.

Ann and Harry exchanged business cards.

Ann: We have a job for you Harry.

Ashley: Harry studied math with Matt. He was in government service but thought that doing mathematical analysis all day long was definitely not what he wanted to do. Harry also saved the life *of a member of our team in another operation with quick thinking. Apparently, Harry carried an ankle Beretta and happened to use it at the right time by shooting an assassin in the shoulder.*

Ann slipped Harry's business card into her Kate Spade wristlet that contained a government issued sidearm.

Ann: *All I can say is that you and your various teams are impressive. Would you like to go over your proposed part of the latest project? That is, if you want to take the assignment that I mentioned.*

Ashley: *I will take it and enjoy it. Matt doesn't know it yet, but I am sure he will support me.*

_____

_____

_____

_____

_____

Scene Four.

The characters are Ashley, Matt, and the General. Director Clark and two intelligence women are mentioned.

Ashley was home and sent an urgent message to Matt and in fifteen minutes, he was standing in front of her. Ashley was beside herself with concern. The scene is their home.

Ashley: *Prince Michael and his son are gone and they want me to retrieve the son. They expect me to pose like a Muslin woman, and retrieve Michael's Prince Philip or whatever he is called. We know that he is a surrogate son, and the Monarchy is totally unaware of that situation.*

Matt: *If you don't want to do it, I'll get you out of it. Don't worry.*

Ashley: *I think you are also part of it.*

Matt. *Holly smoke! I'll ask the General to find out whether or not we are in fact involved. They always contact him first, and then he turns it over to me, whatever the situation.*

Matt was known to keep his cool, often in the most trying conditions. Today was no exception. Matt had another round of golf scheduled with the General, so he decided to wait and see what the General had to say about the kidnapping situation, as it was described by Ashley, even though the description was rather sketchy.

_____

_____

_____

_____

_____

Scene Five.

The characters are Matt and the General. Director Clark is mentioned but does not physically participate in the scene.

Matt is being coy about why their interactions have been strange lately. He senses a problem and wants it to show itself in it's own way.

Matt: *Things have been different lately. I know from past experience that something has come up. You cancelled out this morning and you have never done that before and you have not been very talkative.*

The General: *Well, a few things have come up. I got an urgent call from Director Clark this morning. Actually it was in the middle of the night. There are two major problems, maybe three, dealing with U.S. security: Iran is planning an operation on our shores and we need a person with the technical insight to solve the problem. The second is that Prince Michael is gone, i.e., not there for some reason. This is the second time he has been missing and this time, it is not of his choosing. Katherine Penelope Redford, the retired Queen, has called directly and asked for our help. Actually, she definitely wanted our attention, i.e., you, me, and Ashley. I think primarily, it is you.*

The General hesitated for a few seconds.

The General: *And the third is China, and specifically, what they know about us and what we don't know about them. The President is concerned, Director Clark is concerned, and I am concerned. I really do not know where all of these problems are coming from all at the same time. Prince Michael is associated with two of them and*

China the third. Here is what I think. If we can resolve the Michael situation, I don't know a better word at the moment, I think we can wipe out the first two problems.

Matt: I think we should try to find out what is going on with Ashley. She has been approached by Ann, Clark's wife, and I think she is a loose wire, and she is taking advantage of the fact that her husband is very busy at the moment.

The General: There is this ridiculous notion that 'What Ann wants, Ann gets". Not around here. If we are involved, we are running the show. We can protect ourselves and the country.

I hope that Ashley will be there when we arrive.

Matt: I totally agree with you. Well stated, Sir.

_____

_____

_____

_____

_____

Scene Six.

The characters are Ashley and Ann.

Ashley and Ann are in the car headed to the airport. She receives an announcement of the message system in the Taycan.

Communication System: *Colonel Clark. This is an announcement from HQ. Turn around and return to the household of Professor Miller. The is a direct order.*

Ann turns the Taycan around and heads back to Ashley's house. She starts talking to Ashley.

Ann: *This is a good chance Ashley to fill you in on the plan. We know a lot about you Ashley. We know you had a royal marriage and were married to Prince Michael, whatever a royal marriage is. We recognize that a royal marriage is not the same as a legal marriage and you had a surrogate baby. I am skipping a lot.*

Ann sneezes. She is nervous.

Ann continues: *Michael subsequently attended Oxford at then Queen's request and received a PhD in astrophysics. Prince Michael went to the U.S. to work and returned to the UK under suspicious conditions. He went back to Oxford and directed rather important research on viruses and vaccines. He was awarded a knighthood. He was abducted by a foreign country - we think - and that country is probably Iran, to work on atomic energy or an advance aircraft of some kind. For example, the Russians are supposed to have a hypersonic missile under development and the Chinese are supposed to* have a hypersonic fighter plane, but you never know what is truth and what is propaganda. Michael may have a talent for putting projects together and that is why they are interested in him. We have evidence that Michael is in Iran, who did the abduction. So, we are proceeding in that direction. Actually, the father and the infant were taken at the same time and we have no knowledge if where they are. The infant is for ransom, we think, but you. Never know. The mole can and will help us, so he will blow his cover and have to be returned with the infant and Michael.

Ashley: Where do I fit in, and also Matt and the General.

Ann continues again: Getting qualified people to do the job would be impossible. That is why you and the others were selected. You are all **quick studies**. Do you know what that means?

Ashley: Of course. We learn fast and are not stupid.

Ann for the last time: The three of you will be acquainted with cultural thing about Iran and also the Farsi Language. That will be 3 weeks. You will be brought in as a Russian, and we can get credentials and fly in as Iranian's do. The men have a problem and probably Matt will have to work that out. He will also have to work out how all of you get extracted. We have the knowledge and resources to work that out. For your information, the General has been given a tentative plan for the extraction. Well, you're home. Thanks for the opportunity to drive such a nice car. To be honest with you, this is not my kind of work. The Director is on travel status and I am just trying to help out. The President gets nervous, the Director gets nervous, and that is why we would like to depend on Matt. The General also gets nervous but is an excellent organizer. All that is left are you and Matt to sort out the big problem, what ever that is. I don't think you are in trouble, but if I inadvertently cause you a problem, I'm sorry. You are a very nice person.

_____

_____

_____

_____

_____

Scene Seven.

The characters are the General, Matt, Ashley, and Ann.

All of the characters arrive at Matt and Ashley's home at about the same time and convene in the living room. Ashley and Ann get there slightly before and arrange the seating. Ann immediately took over the leader ship role and irritated Matt and Ashley beyond belief. The leadership business by Ann will have to end now, thought Matt. The General runs our show. Matt looked over at Ashley, and it was obvious that she felt the same way. People generally think that their way is the right way, except for the Army way that they say is superior, except for the General officers. There is also a a General's way. The General interrupted Ann in her first sentence and, from then on, it was the General's show.

The General: *We are all here for a common cause. Some important people are missing and we are obligated to find them. I have a note and a big plan. I do not who made it. I repeat, I do not know whom made it. In addition to the missing people, there are military grade weapons that are superior to those of then U.S. there are exercises going on over then Sea of Taiwan's, and the Russians say they have fighter plane that is superior to then F-35. So we have plenty to do.*

Ann: *We can't solve all of the problems at one time. Which do we cover first?*

The General: *It is the missing person or persons. England is involved in it, and the former Queen has contacted me personally. We will have Buzz Bunday working that end. I haven't talked to him personally. Prince Michael, the Oxford scientist, has been abducted. We don't know for sure, as of now, that he is in Iran, probably against his wishes. He has a child with the former Princess that has been under the care of a Duke and Duchess of one of the Royal Kingdoms, and he is also missing. Both events took place at the same time, and the authorities believe they are related. We will solve there other problems when we get to them.*

Matt: *Iran is a big place.*

Ashley: *Michael is practically useless. His only asset is his extreme intellectual capability. He lead the team that created the British vaccine during the pandemic.*

Ann: *Why would anyone abduct a young boy?*

The General: *Ransome. The Iranians are short of cash, as a nation, since the U.S. has cut off their cash flow in international markets.*

Matt: *Let's make a plan. As far as Michael is concerned, I see a few obvious problems, such as locating him, getting the persons that will do the extraction, and transportation in and out. We'll have to coordinate with Director Clark on this matter. It's going to be a very big and complicated job. It will cost someone a very large amount of money.*

The General: *Okay, Matt and I will take care of Michael, and Ann and Ashley will take care of Michael's missing boy that has been named*

Philip George William Charles by the British Monarchy. I've talked to Director Clark and he has government generated information on the subject. At this point, the group will disband. We will work as team and the government has unique plans on how to we should proceed.

Matt and the General arrange to meet with the Director of Intelligence in Langley in two days.

Scene Eight.

The characters are Director Mark Clark, Matt, and the General.

The trio are meeting in intelligence direction facilities. Matt and the General have flown in for a meeting with Mark Clark. The men are seated in a sophisticated government room.

Director Clark: *Thanks for an early start, Gentlemen. I run a tight ship. There is a lot of work to be done around here, and too few people.*

The General: *It doesn't matter, Mark. We are used to getting out on the golf course early, so we are used to it.*

Director Clark: *You already know the drill. I am going to focus on the available resources, since you are familiar with what's going on in the country. I may give some suggestions because we - the agency - have been working on the situation.*

Matt: *We want to get Prince Michael out of Iran, and you might know that is where he is. You probably have a connection, and I guess it is that Iranian guy from Hilton Head, who couldn't get anything right.*

Director Clark: *It is, and it is a direct result of your intelligence work.*

The General: *Do you want us to leave a strong message when we exit from Iran?*

Director Clark: *If you mean destruction of some kind, then the answer is 'yes'. We can't show very much power by just getting out of the place. We have open DOD contracts with almost all contractors including the Lehman Corporation. You have the complete resources of the United States and the allies with whom we are affiliated. The ball is totally in your hands. My wife Ann will interact with you on matters associated with the Royal baby named Prince Philip and subsequent assistance and actions involving the State of Israel.*

Matt: *Do we have access to facilities such as the military drone network?*

Director Clark: *You do. Why do you ask?*

Matt: *An idea just popped into my mind. I just wondered if they - referring to Iran - electronically monitor drones like they monitor traditional enemy aircraft entering their airspace.*

Director Clark: *They do not. Apparently, they think that since drones are slow and can be easily identified visually, protection from them is not necessary. They might be correct, since drones are tactically harmless.*

The General: *I feel this is an operation with the highest priority to our nation and should be analyzed carefully.*

Clark waited for the General to say something more, but apparently the General was finished.

Director Clark: *It is of the highest priority and it has been planned more carefully than anything we have done in recent years. You are* expected at the White House, and Kenneth Strong, the President, will make himself immediately available to you. A car will take you to the airfield, a White House jet to Dulles, and the a Marine One helicopter to the White House. I'm sorry I have a President Daily Brief (PDB) meeting, and we have a strict deadline, so I have to stick around here.

Both Matt and the General look impressed.

_____

_____

_____

_____

Scene Nine.

The characters are the President of the United States, Matt, the General, and Kimberly Scott.

The scene is the President's private office.

The President: *Greetings gentlemen. We have an important subject to discuss. But first, how have your lives been?*

Both Matt and the General just smiled. No answer was expected.

The President: *I have an important job for you and your team. An important incident has occurred for which we need your assistance. Prince Michael of England has been abducted, and I have received a personal call on the subject from each of the following: the King of the United Kingdom, the former queen HRH Kathrine Penelope Radford, the Prime Minister of England, and the U.S. Secretary of State. You already know the problem that we must find him and return him to England in perfect health.*

The President hesitated, as if to say. 'These guys know this already. Why am I here?' I could be eating breakfast.

The President: *Our primary ally is the United Kingdom, and our good relations with them depend on it. I need immediate attention and every resource in the world, under our control, is available.*

Matt: *Do we have a description of what has been accomplished so far? A few items have been mentioned, but the totality of the preliminary work must be much more than that. For example, we've* *heard several times that the Prince and his young son are in Iran. Is this assessment for sure true?*

The President: *Mark Clark, Director of Intelligence, has our results. All I do is to motivate people and pay the bills.*

The General: *Deadlines?*

The President looked as if to say, 'Is this guy that dumb?' He hesitated. Matt looked off to the side, as if he wasn't there. Emphasize this for realism.

The President: *ASAP. There is no need to mention again how important this is. You guys are on your own. You are professionals. Just do your job.*

Somewhat irritated, the President got up and left the private office through the secret exit. He did not say a word.

Matt: *Let's get out of here. Enough has been said.*

Matt and the General wound their way to Marine One and back to Langley. The General tried to call Clark but was told he was on travel status. He was informed there was a packet of information on the project named ESCAPE, available through an analyst name Kimberly Scott. Kimberly was abrupt with the General when she was asked for the packet by the General.

Director decision: *Matt explain to Kimberly that the General was a war hero, and also getting older. For the first time, Matt realized that the General might be getting a little older, and he would have to compensate by carrying more of the burden. This should be evidenced by his behavior.*

_____

_____

_____

_____

_____

Scene Ten.

The characters are Matt and the General.

On the flight from Langley to New Jersey, Matt is the Captain and the General is the First Officer. In the modern world, this means that Matt was flying their small plane. The General was sitting in the co-pilot's seat was fast asleep. Matt had the small plane on auto and was thinking through the task at hand. He had a small notebook and was taking down notes. The scene changes dynamically from the airplane to a small office in Ashley and Matt's home. The General's housekeeper doesn't have a clearance.

The General wakes up.

Matt: *I took a few notes on our flight and I wonder what you think of them. Do you want to hear what I wrote down?*

The General: *I sure do. You are good at developing creative ideas. You are really outstanding at it. I'm better at planning and organizing. It comes with age. I know it.*

Matt: *At this point, we have knowledge of the problem and the U.S. resources, since we have Kimberly Scott. Some of the U.S. drones are designed and built at the Lehman Company, located in Seattle - especially the big drones. My idea is to have Lehman design and develop a manned drone, just like the one used in combat without the people. Sounds crazy, but I think it will work. The manned drones would fly over Iran and deliver a couple of agents to the ground - namely, you and me, disguised as Iranians. Perhaps, we might have* to fast rope to the ground, but in either case we would be there. We could land in the Sukhoi air field, the one we have used before. Iran ordered a fleet of fighter planes from Russia and built a special field for them. Then Iran experienced a budget problem, because the U.S. blocked their bank funds, and the order was cancelled. The field - the runways and buildings - are unused and totally accessible.

The General: *I remember the air field.*

Matt: *We will learn the whereabout of Prince Michael through Atalus, who is now a U.S. mole. He is the Iranian terrorizer leader named Adam Benfield that was uncovered and is now a spy for the U.S. Subsequently, a manned drone, probably the same one, will pick up Prince Michael, the young infant, Ashley, Benfield, and both of us and transport us to Israel, and then on to our respective countries. We take Benfield because his cover will probably be known. We need information on the English individuals that are to be abducted from Iran, if there are any, and we can get that from Buzz Bunday in England. The biggest problem is together a drone modified - or built - by the Lehman Company in Seattle. It makes the unmanned version and could revise it for manned occupants.*

The General: *Lehman is not exactly waiting for us to request a whole aircraft, and it takes time to design and build things.*

Matt: *First, you must have heard that Lehman has an extensive workshop that can make any part in anyone of its products. They have been able to do so because they use subcontractors and, once in a while, they are delinquent. If a bomber plane, for example, is one day late, Lehman is fined a million dollars. It is true. Lehman has never had to pay it. The U.S. government is a tough customer, hence* the extensive machine shop. So, they can do it; all we have to do is determine what we want done. And, of course, they will figure out how to do it.

The General: *We have the contract information through Kimberly Scott. I think you have used her before.*

_____

_____

_____

_____

_____

Scene Eleven.

The characters are Matt, the General, Ashley, and Kimberly Scott. Kimberly Scott is unseen.

The group is seated in the living room of Matt and Ashley's home. Matt is holding his satellite phone; he has just contacted Kimberly.

Matt: *Hello Kimberly. This is Matt. Are you free to talk. I'm here at home with Ashley and the General.*

Kimberly: *I was expecting a call from you. I have a packet for you, deposited by a high-level group under the command of Director Clark. You are going to be surprised. I'm send you all of the information, but I can summarize it for you over the phone. Things have changed. First and foremost, the Lehman company has changed dramatically. They are running under control of AI, and practically everything is now automated. I'm not sure that you will like it. It was a total surprise to us.*

Matt: *Let's have it. It's better now than later.*

Kimberly: *They brought in a system called Stategate that runs the place now. Actually, Stategate brought itself in and runs the entire company. The management of the company tells Stategate what it wants to do and wherever to go, and Stategate figures out what to do and where to go. I feed that information into Stategate, after you tell me. If I am not here, you have to feed the information into a computer that simulates me. The company is a very large assembly line. If you want something and Stategate has it, it tells you where you can obtain* it. You can also tell it what to do. If it doesn't have it, it will tell you how long it will take to make it, and where and when to pick up the result. Make a request and I will give you the place you can pick up the item. Generally, you have to tell it where and what you want to do with the result. Don't worry. It has safeguards. I'll stay on the line. Just work out what you want and I'll give you a quick response.

Matt addresses Ashley and the General.

Matt: *If we want a manned drone, quick give me an answer. We can change it. She didn't say, but we can assume the system takes care of changes. After all, we are humans.*

The General: *We need a large manned drone, piloted by a human and copilot. Conventional seating.*

Ashley: *Add one baby seat.*

Matt: *Seats for The General, Ashley, Me, Prince Michael, Benfield, another mole, helper - probably Harry Stevens, plus baby and pilots. That came to 7 plus 2 pilots plus baby seats. One extra seat. Delivery to where? Israel drone base. Linear take off. Do we need an escort?*

The General: *Probably a F-117A supersonic based in an aircraft carrier with a AMRAAM rocket. Average kill distance of 5 miles. Complete destruction of the enemy. Just in case.*

Kimberly: *I heard all of that and I ran it as a test case. You can have one unit and a backup in the drone base in 4 weeks from the go signal plus 2 days familiarization. One more thing. Delivery is by 2 Jumbo C-17s. Another thing. No changes after 2 weeks. Is that it?*

Matt: *Is that a go, everyone?*

Everyone nodded in the affirmative.

Kimberly: *I can't see you Matt. Is that a yes?*

Matt: *Yes, it is a yes.*

Kimberly: *Good job team. You are on your way. Godspeed.*

Everyone was totally surprised.

The General: *Dinner at the Green Room? Let me ask Stategate. Just kidding.*

Scene Twelve.

The characters in this scene are Kimberly (unseen), Matt, Ashley, and the General.

The team of Matt, Ashley, and the General are gathered in the living room of Matt and Ashley's house. Matt calls Kimberly.

Matt: *Good morning Kimberly, how are things in Washington?*

Kimberly: *Things are fine here, the weather is good and my work load is light today. You have only one item left on your plan. Would you like for me to give you a heads up?*

Matt: *Yes. Just read it out loud, and then we will be on our way to Iran training.*

Kimberly: *The two training courses on Iranian affairs are essentially the same, except for the male and female segments. The first two weeks are a condensed version of the Farsi language, and everyday customs. The third week involves personal interactions. The lectures are hand on and the language is totally immersive, as are religious and social sectors. Methods of dressing and socio-personal relations are described in great detail. The days are organized to be long, tedious, and complicated. Practice sessions are involved as are living conditions. Living in Iran is quite pleasurable provided that a person behaves by the rules and has something to offer the country through intellect and basic knowledge. Computer skills could be quite profitable since the general knowledge of technology is not widespread. The male and female segments are totally different. The male segment covers military, government procedures, and social behavior. The female* segment focuses on female dress, child care, and subservience in a closed society. The American courses are given in Nebraska for men and in Virginia's for women use mock ups of Iranian structure and operation.

Good luck to you guys, Matt, Ashley, and then General. You will be changed people.

The three crusaders walk slowly off the set.

_____

_____

_____

_____

_____

Scene Thirteen.

The characters are Matt, the General, and a lone student passer-by.

Matt and the General are dressed as Iranians and walking down the Main Street of the university town. They walked about one block, when they are interrupted by a student.

Student: *Excuse me Sir, are you related to Dr. Miller in the math department?*

Matt: *Yes, I'm his cousin and live in California. Just here for a family affair.*

Student: *You sure look like him.*

The General: *That was fast thinking.*

Matt: *Thanks. It was pretty cool. I have to admit.*

The General: *Do we have an escort for Ashley when she goes to Iran?*

Matt: *In the plan, it mentioned that Harry Steven would be the escort. Apparently, the former Queen Katherine Penelope Radford has selected him. That was the first I heard about that. I heard that Adam Benfield would have a female mole to take care of of her in Iran and escort her with the kid - I mean baby - to the pickup at the Sukhoi airport. She was that extra seat that Kimberly recorded. It's possible that Harry is to escort Ashley to Tehran and then return. Then the* *female mole would take over. It seems that everything is okay. Harry can then travel to the Drone base in preparation for the retraction.*

The General: *This is the most complicated project we have been on. We still have the Iran internals to work on. I think that is our job.*

Matt: *It is also a bit risky. We are going to need the help of Adam Benfield.*

_____

_____

_____

_____

_____

Scene Fourteen.

The characters are Matt and Ashley.

After three strenuous weeks, Ashley and Matt met at their home. Both were glad to see each other. They were in a risky operation and both were on edge.

Ashley: *Are you going to play golf?*

Matt: *No, I'm going to spend as much time as possible at home with you. We will have a short time - possibly three days - and I want them to be worthwhile. Are you having any operational problems with your end.*

Ashley: *No, not even one. We will take a direct flight to London in three days and Atalus with the help of an associate will get me to the son. Then, a fast Mercedes S500 will take us to an airport - they call it the Sukhoi Airfield where a U.S. drone will pick us up. The two teams will meet in our flight in the drone to the Israel drone base. We will then board a fast military plane to London and meet up with Katherine Penelope Redford and the rest of the people in the Monarchy. I will relay the result of our operation to Kimberly Scott, and she will arrange a flight back to the states. That is what I've heard anyway.*

Matt: *That's essentially the same with us, except the target is Prince Michael. I heard from Kimberly Scott that Buzz will take care of everything in the return to the states. That's good enough for me.*

Ashley: *He's quite a guy.*

Matt: *He should be. He's getting $4 million, if not more, for his efforts.*

Ashley: *What about us?*

Matt: *The General said we should get at least $4 million, but probably more if the President is pleased beyond reason and the retired Queen is also pleased. I think they will be.*

Ashley: *I will be too.*

_____

_____

_____

_____

_____

Scene Fifteen.

The only character in this scene is Matt. He talks to Buzz Bunday, who is only a voice.

The satellite call between Matt and Buzz is to double check that they are all on the same page. Several people were involved with making the master plan.

Matt: *Greeting Buzz. This is Matt calling to double check the operational details of the project.*

Buzz: *Glad you called Matt. I was getting a little worried, This operation is a big deal around here. The Monarch is like a leaky sponge. The retired Queen is involved. We are going to use Russian passports for Ashley and your man Harry Steven's. Isn't that a misspelling?*

Matt: *It's legit, Buzz. He's dependable, and sharp as a tick. He was an intelligence analyst but prefers action.*

Buzz: *Before we start, we turned this guy Atalus. He prefers the name Adam Benfield. He is your key person in Iran. Okay. Harry escorts Ashley on the flight to Tehran. Benfield has a female mole escort Ashley to where ever she is to reside. Benfield says he has that covered. To him, that means he has taken care of it. The female mole will introduce us the kid. Okay, Prince Philip. Harry flies back to then states. This a passport game. Harry uses Russian for Iran and American to get back into the States. Is this satisfactory, so far.*

Matt: *Perfect so far.*

Buzz: *Harry flies back o the Sates and flies with you and the General to the secret Israel drone base. We use the General's Gulfstream. We have secured the two F22 pilots somebody mentioned. When we have a completed mission, it will be used for Israel to London transit and London to the States transport. Where are the drones and why do you have two of them?*

Matt: *The two drones will arrive the same day as 'we the people.'*

Buzz: *Why do you need two of them?*

Matt: *One is a decoy.*

A long pause.

Buzz: *How long do we wait there for you to return.*

Matt: *Don't know exactly. Probably less that 5 days. Could be 2.*

Buzz: *Anything else?*

Matt: *That's all from this end. You don't have to ask. The General mentioned 3 but I am giving you 4, plus a possible bonus from the Queen. I'm using U.S. dollars.*

Buzz: *Is it that much? Are you sure?*

Matt: *I'm sure Buzz. Thanks for your help.*

Buzz: *It's a pleasure Matt. Signing off.*

\
\

\

\
\

Scene Sixteen.

The characters are Ashley, Harry, Matt, and the General.

The groups were scheduled to leave at the same time from Newark International. Ashley and Harry were taking Lufthansa to London, with a one hour layover and then on to Tehran. They were scheduled to pick up their Russian passports from Buzz in London City Airport and then on to Tehran. Matt and the General were flying directly to the secret Israel drone base in the General's Gulfstream, fitted with long distant travel features. The General had secured the two former F-22 pilots.

The four travelers take a limo to the airport. The stage is set to look like a limo.

Matt: *I can hardly believe that we are actually on our way.*

Ashley: *I can believe it. This Iranian woman's costume is already driving me crazy. People will look at me. This is worse than terrible.*

Harry: *What about me, escorting a Muslim woman?*

Matt: *You should have stayed in school and got your PhD.*

Harry: *You did and you are just 5 feet away from me.*

The General: *I wish Anna were here to tell me that everything will turn out just fine.*

Harry: *Do we have food on this flight? I'm hungry already. You guys will get American food in Iran. They copy American with hamburgers and beer. I'm going on to Israel and I don't know about the food there. I'm sure they don't copy.*

The General: *There is plenty of food. Just go back and get it. The government isn't paying for a stewardess. Matt! Did you bring a math book?*

Matt: *Of course. You know me.*

The passengers were tired and soon fell asleep.

_____

_____

_____

_____

Scene Seventeen.

The characters are Matt, the General, and Adam Benfield, also known as Atalus.

Matt and the General have ridden in the manned drone to Sukhoi Aid Field and were met by Adam Benfield in his new Mercedes S550 car. The men were pleased to meet each other, even though they had met previously on Hilton Head Island in South Carolina. Matt and the General were totally surprised. Their friend Atalus, as he was known, was the biggest failure in Iran's history, and here he is driving a Mercedes car to pick up spies. The General and Benfield are on friendly terms. All three are in the car.

The General: *Adam, what is going on? Here you are, picking up a couple of illegal people in a new Mercedes car?*

Benfield: *We Iranians are rich. I guess you didn't know that. Do you remember the Shah of Iran, as he was called. Those people that worked for Iran were suitably rewarded. Things have changed, but the internal structure remains. The shah took the advice of an excellent American Scholar who is now the President of a university with his name.*

The General: *I think that I know who he is referring to. I got my Master of Science in Computer Science there. I later worked with him on a business venture - that is - the President, not the Shah.*

Matt: *Now we know. It's a small world.*

Benfield: *I'm going to take you to our most luxurious hotel and pick you up at 7:00 am. We start early in Iran. Tomorrow, I will take you to Prince Michael. He is working on the pandemic epidemic - pardon my French, as they say in America - and is helping us develop a vaccine. The virus is a very big problem here, since there are no countries that will help us.*

Matt: *Now that is a surprise. We were told by our American intelligence sources that he was working on an atomic project, or something like that.*

The General: *Now the abduction makes sense.*

Benfield: *You may order what you want from room service. They like American food here. Even hamburgers and beer.*

_____

_____

_____

_____

_____

Scene Eighteen.

The characters are Matt, the General, Benfield, Prince Michael.

Benfield picks up Matt and the General and the scene evolves into a conference room. Benfield arrives at 7:00 am. It is only a few miles to the conference room.

Benfield: *Have you had breakfast?*

The General: *We haven't. We slept late. It had been a long day for us.*

Benfield: *Pity. Our food is the best in the world. We copy. It is only a few miles to the biology research building. Every project has a building.*

The three enter a conference room that is practically empty. Benfield introduces Matt and the General to a few biological scientists, and Matt and the General get to use their Farsi. No one seems to be interested in them.

Benfield: *The scientists are Swiss. They act like they are better than everyone. They might be.*

In fifteen minutes or so, Prince Michael enters with two body guards and starts to lecture in English. The audience seems to understand English.

Matt and the General look at each other. Matt makes eye contact with Prince Michael, who recognizes Matt and flicks his eye. Matt and the Prince know each other.

The Prince's lecturer on viral science is well-prepared and very technical; it is not clear that the audience understands what is going on.

Matt: *I was talking to a guy who was assembling an Artificial Intelligence development group for a company in Switzerland, and he was interviewing people for his team. A young fellow introduced himself and said he wild like to be on the team. The AI asked him what he had done in AI, and the person responded that he had no experience and wasn't even sure what AI was. His boss had asked who was interested in AI and he came over. Maybe the men in the room are just interested.*

The General: *Could be the case.*

_____

_____

_____

_____

_____

Scene Nineteen.

The characters are Benfield, Matt, the General, and Robert Peterson. Peterson is from Iran and has studied in the U.S.

The next morning, Benfield repeated the trip to the biology building with Matt and the General. The room was empty except for the trio. They were approached by a tall Iranian officer. He addressed the General.

Peterson: *Excuse me, do I know you? Did we attend the university together?*

The General looked at the officer and said.

The General: *Yes, you do. We were in the same master's class together. You were from Iran and your name is …*

The General thought for a few seconds.

The General: *You are Robert Peterson, and your associate was John Evans, and you were both from Iran.*

Peterson: *That is true. My Iran name is different. I am the country's technology officer, equivalent to an American Vice President. I would like to talk to you.*

Matt recognized that their cover has been blown. He looked blank, but his brain went into high gear. He thought: we are in big trouble, real big trouble. I wonder about this guy Benfield. I am going to have to figure out a way of getting out of those situation. Matt was as cool as a cucumber.

The three men were escorted by a guard to a separate room. The Iranian officer initiated the conversation.

Peterson: *My American studies enabled me to attain my high position. I can have you put in prison or even executed.*

The General swallowed and cleared his throat. Matt looked into his eyes and saw fear. To the Director: the audience knows it is going to turn out okay and perhaps a little humor would be in order. Accordingly, the General's pants are wet and it was even visible. It's a play, not real life.

Matt: *We are here to extract Prince Michael. He was taken without his wishes by an agency in Iran.*

Peterson: *I know. I had it done.*

Matt: *Why didn't you ask him to be a consultant to your country?*

Peterson: *That is not the way thongs are done in Iran. In have no control over that.*

Peterson hesitated several seconds.

Peterson continues: *I have A PhD in mathematics from a university in California. I know of you. You are a string theory scholar. You are Matt Miller.*

The General: *Why did you do this?*

Peterson: *Our country is dying from the COVID virus, as you call it, and no country will provide us with a vaccine. We can pay for it.*

The General was totally flustered. Matt was still as cool as a cucumber.

Matt: *Can we make a deal?*

Peterson: *All options are open.*

Matt: *Can you exchange the four of us - The General, your friend Atalus, Prince Michael, and me - for a working vaccine for all of your country.*

Peterson: *I can do anything. I have the power to release you as soon as you guarantee the vaccine.*

Peterson was cool as a cucumber. The General has an amazed look. Must be the mathematics.

Matt: *I can give you an answer in minutes. If you can direct me outdoors, where I can make a satellite call to the U.S.A.*

Matt called Kimberly Scott on his wrist satellite phone. Kimberly understood the plan in seconds.

Kimberly: *We have plenty of vaccine. Let me call President Strong.*

Kimberly responded in five minutes.

Kimberly: *He will guarantee the vaccine free of charge to Iran if England will guarantee a nominal amount. Iran has 80 million people. 60 millions are adults. We will guarantee 40 million if England will guarantee 20 million. As a side comment, he will guarantee all 60 million, if necessary. He felt that England should give a little. After* all, this guy Michael is from England. I have to call Sir Bunday and he can contact the Prime Minister. Just give me a few minutes. Just a minute. I have a response. England will guarantee 20 million doses. The following is important to complete the transaction. We expect to transfer the vaccine in refrigerated trucks loaded into C17s. We can load our 40 million doses into two refrigerated trucks in one C17 and England can load their 20 million doses into one C17. The three trucks in two C-17s will be delivered to Iran to land at Sukhoi Airfield in two weeks - probably 10 days. Iran has to guarantee they will do diligence and provide sufficient medical staff handle the does of vaccine. We will provide two doctors and one nurse to train them. Who is your contact in Iran?

Matt: Dr. Robert Peterson. He is VP of technology for the entire country, and educated in the States. What about the kids?

Kimberly: The President said that we will guarantee child support as it becomes necessary. Oh, one more thing. If two U.S. doctors and one nurse are insufficient, we will supplement that aspect of the agreement. So far, kids in Iran have not been affected.

Kimberly: We have Peterson in our database. By the way, this Sir Charles Bunday, known as Buzz, is a wonder. I asked him how much he is getting for his work. He said $4 million and I raised it to $5 million.

Matt: You're a genius and a nice person.

Kimberly: I know. Just doing my job. I hope to meet you. Some day.

Matt returned to the separate room.

Matt: *Listen please. I have very good news. The united State and England have agreed to provide 60 million does of vaccine to the country of Iran. It will be loaded into 3 refrigerated trucks that will be transferred to Iran in 2 C-17 heavy duty aircraft. Two doctors and one nurse will also accompany the vaccine to assist the Iranian medical staff. It should arrive in 10 days at Suzhoi Airfield. Dr, Robert Peterson will be the key person in the transaction.*

Matt, the General, Dr. Peterson, and Benfield, known in Iran as Atalus, all shook hands. The operation of the American team had done its job.

_____

_____

_____

_____

_____

Scene Twenty.

This is a unique end to a play.

The characters are Ashley, Master Philip, and her female Iran escort were picked up in their luxurious quarters and to be transferred to Sukhoi Airfield. The occurs on the first day of the holy season.

The scene is without voice and depicts 3 persons entering a Mercedes sedan headed to Sukhoi Airfield.

At approximately the same time, Prince Michael, Matt, the General, and Benfield were picked up in another Mercedes

The second scene is without voice and depicts 4 passengers headed to the same location.

The third scene depicts Harry Steevens loading the 7 passengers into a drone.

The fourth scene, again without words, depicts 7 passengers and Harry unloading the drone in the Israel drone base.

All of the passengers wave to the audience and all yell 'Thank You. We couldn't have done it without you."

_____

_____

_____

_____

_____

ABOUT THIS PLAY

The play is an adaption of the accompanying novel entitled The Final Escape. The book and the play are all fictional. Absolutely nothing really exists and it is totally for entertainment.

The play is fungible. That means that it composition may and can be modified under the usual circumstances with stage plays. The three associated publications are:

The Final Escape book
The Stage Play of The Final Escape
The Script of The Final Escape

The The Final Escape book is intended for the producer and the director. The Stage Play of The Final Escape is intended for the director. The The Script of The Final Escape is for the characters. The script and its format are intended to be reproduced.

Three blank lines accompany each scene for obvious reasons. This applied only to the script. The play is written with the characters in mind. Some sequences are a little long. But actors are smart people in addition to being good looking, and can easily handle them.

The subject matter contains no sex, no violence, and no bad language. It is realistic in the presentation. It is suitable for general audiences, college plays, and high school productions.

This particular volume contains actors scripts. Actor segments are in italics typeface.

ABOUT THE AUTHOR

The author is a professor who has also worked for Boeing, Oak Ridge National Laboratory, and IBM. He has written computer science books, business books, and several novels.

He is an avid runner and has competed 94 marathons, including Boston13 times and New York 14 times. He and his wife have lived in Switzerland where he was a consultant and a professor specializing in Artificial Intelligence.

He loves plays and sees every one he gets the chance. New York and London are his favorite venues. Mousetrap is his favorite play.

A Few Books by Harry Katzan Jr.

Advanced Lessons in Artificial Intelligence

Conspectus of Artificial Intelligence

Artificial Intelligence is a Service

Strategy and AI

The Money Gate

The Money Affair

END OF THE BOOK

The Script of
The FINAL ESCAPE
In Three Acts

Printed in the United States
by Baker & Taylor Publisher Services

Printed in the United States
by Baker & Taylor Publisher Services